FABULOUS FIFI
THE FLAMENCO FLAMINGO!

To Dan, Elfie and Sasha - AC

To the memory of my beloved father RK,
who taught me how to have my head in the clouds
while keeping my feet on the ground - IK

ISBN:978-1-913339-03-6
Text copyright – Alice Corrie 2021
Illustrations copyright – Ipek Konak 2021

Alice Corrie & Ipek Konak

FABULOUS FIFI

THE FLAMENCO FLAMINGO!

First published in the UK 2021 by Owlet Press

www.owletpress.com

Fifi wanted to be
fabulous!

Fifi wanted to be **fantastic!**

And most of all,
Fifi wanted to be **famous!**

But . . .

. . . she was just an
itty-bitty,
teeny-tiny,
fluffy
flamingo!

Fifi felt small in the colossal colony of flamingos.

She wanted to stand out from the crowd.
She wanted to show them that
she was a flamingo worth noticing!

But . . .

. . . she was just an
itty–bitty,
teeny-tiny,
fluffy,
flappy
flamingo!

Fifi wanted to **dance!**
She wanted **drama** and **dresses.**
And most of all, she wanted to be . . .

Fifi, the Flamenco Flamingo,
the most **famous** flamingo in the world!

But . . .

. . . she was just an

itty-bitty,

teeny-tiny,

fluffy, flappy,

flippy-floppy

flamingo!

Fifi didn't know the first thing about flamenco dancing.
But she could stomp her feet and flap and twirl.

That would be a start!

So she **stomped** her feet,

flapped her wings

and **twirled** round and round.

But . . .

. . . she was just an

itty-bitty, teeny-tiny, **flappy, flippy-floppy, wibbly-wobbly flamingo!**

HA HA!

Ha ha!

HA HA!

HAHA!

And her dancing was a **disaster!**

She landed on her bottom with her long, lanky legs waving in the air.
All the other flamingos fell about laughing and told Fifi her dancing
wasn't **fabulous** or **fantastic**
and that it certainly **wasn't** going to make her famous!

Fifi felt like a failure, just an

itty-bitty, teeny-tiny, **flappy,
flippy-floppy,
wibbly-wobbly,
fed up
flamingo!**

Maybe she should stick to what she knew.

Live a normal life.

Blend in.

Be happy with what she had.

But she had a **dream** to be . . .

...Fifi, the Flamenco Flamingo,

the most **famous** flamingo in the world!

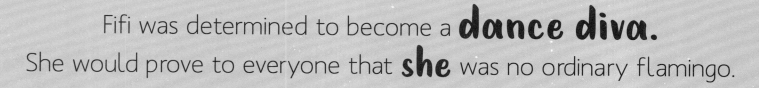

Fifi was determined to become a **dance diva.**
She would prove to everyone that **she** was no ordinary flamingo.

Fifi flew far and wide.

Across the lake,

the hills and the city.

And **then** she saw her chance . . .

... the Flamenco Fiesta!

This was the place for Fifi.

She was **mesmerised** by the music.
She was **dazzled** by the dresses,
the **dancers**
and the **drama!**

And she knew that **this** was **her moment** to become a . . .

... frolicking, famous, Flamenco Flamingo!

Fifi landed on the stage.

She **stomped** her feet and **flapped** her wings.

She twirled round and round and honked her honk,
trying with all her might to be a . . .

fantastic,
frolicking,
famous,
Flamenco
Flamingo!

And even though
Fifi's style was
a little funny . . .

Fifi **honked** with joy.
Finally, she was a . . .

Go FiFi!

Honk!

Honk!

Honk!

flawless, fantastic,
frolicking, famous,
Flamenco Flamingo!

Fifi had **drama** and more dresses than she could count!
She travelled the world with her **amazing** act . . .

DR

LONDON

AWAR

the
fabulous,
flawless, fantastic,
frolicking, famous

Fifi, the Flamenco Flamingo!

FIFI

PARIS

PISA

FIRST SHOW

Fifi's dream had finally come true.
She was the most famous flamingo in the world –

a fashionable,
fabulous, flawless, fantastic,
frolicking, famous . . .

FLAMENCO

FLAMINGO!

OWLET PRESS

Growing into wisdom

Discover even more stories to treasure!

That splashy, magical mermaid, wherever can she be? Join our intrepid family to find out! In this underwater adventure, readers will enjoy trying to find the hiding mermaid, while meeting magical endangered wildlife on the way.

RRP: £7.99

The next time you look up at the night sky, you might see the sparkling metal planet with all its robots and their robo-babies.
A story about all the ways babies arrive into their families like IVF, surrogacy, donors and adoption.

RRP: £7.99

In the 'Polka Dot Pet Shop', where every animal is magical and marvellous, we find a plain, brown mouse who struggles to see how he fits in. Young readers learn about confidence, as the mouse realises his own unique talents.

RRP: £7.99